EVINCEPUB PUBLISHING

Parijat Extension, Bilaspur, Chhattisgarh 495001

First Published by Evincepub Publishing 2020

Copyright © Liliyan Swarna Kalai 2020

All Rights Reserved.

ISBN: 978-93-89988-60-4

Wind Chimes

Liliyan Swarna Kalai

ABOUT THE BOOK

'Wind Chimes' is a collection of poems written by Liliyan Swarna Kalai. The period of the work is from when the author was 18 years old. A variety of themes form this compilation that would interest readers of all age group. Animals and birds, flora and fauna find place in this book. A few poems might interest the romantically inclined. You will also find life's challenges, emotional ordeal, and moments of celebrations, magical and spiritual reflections

Like the chimes that softly jingle in the breeze, these poems would stir your thoughts and caress your soul. Open your minds and thoughts that are reflections of everyday events like a lost pet, college life, long lost friends, an urban garden and so on that passes by so quickly in the journey of life.

ABOUT THE AUTHOR

The author Dr. Liliyan Swarna Kalai is a professional Social Worker with a PhD in environmental concerns. An English graduate from Madras Christian College, Chennai, she did her masters of Social Work in Madras School of Social work. After serving the Spastic Society of Tamil Nadu for a couple of years, she joined the Chennai Metropolitan Development Authority as Community Officer working for the Economically Weaker Sections in the field of Housing, Environmental Issues and so on. Her work involved projects of the World Bank, United Nations Development Programme and in the later years being a nodal officer for the Right to Information of the Tamil Nadu government.

At present, the author is serving as a consultant in an NGO (Krupa) which works among the gypsies, bonded labourers, prisoners and their families. Writing had been a passion from college days. Commitment at work, family responsibilities and pursuing a doctorate degree had a setback in writing for soul satisfaction. Nevertheless, she has published technical papers, articles and reports of good standing for the UN, TN Govt and Universities. It was always at the back of her mind to publish all that has been saved in her laptop and diaries. And so here goes the first chapter.

She has passion for English Pop, Tamil movie songs and Spiritual songs. The author has travelled widely and has visited fourteen countries in Europe, USA and Asia. Evince Publishers has accepted to help her realize the long lasting dream.

FOREWORD

Poets are artistic personalities in general, but sp [specifically highly sensitive. They are sure to feel a state of changes ten times clearer than others. And most of them find a great inspiration in poetic manifestations. So some those unusually distinct their own feelings represented in the form of rhymed words which are gathered for valuable readers' choice and pleasure.

Poetry is an interpretation of realistic life through human imagination and feelings The world with which science deals is what we commonly say as the world of facts and figures' by which we properly mean the world of physical actuality objectively considered and followed. It is the business of a scientist, unlike that of a poet. A real poet will always visualize of the real things into an aesthetic perspective in life

Poetry grow directly out of life is of course to articulate that it is in life itself that we have to seek the sources of inspiration, or, in other words, the impulses which have given birth in the divine form of celestial poetic expressions. The below lines are true example for of the poet's own good thoughts in life.

"*The contents were simple, cheerful and good*
Lucid to convey the matter, as it should.
Very soon the new book would turn weary and old
Even the clear lines will be covered by mould.
Unaware of the votes it polled
It stayed put in the household..." (The Unread Book)

A poem is often read for its message that it carries. The message is generally obscured in the background of the true poem, sometimes; it is difficult because its language that is used is often indirect with the ordinary reader. There is no limit of subjects that can be used in a poem.

They could be written about the beauty of nature, birds, seasons like spring and the most commonly known theme, love. Poetry is a form of literature which can be used to express with vivid thoughts and feelings from the poet's own perspective. Honorable Poet Dr. Liliyan Swarna Kalai emphasis this thought in this book "Wind Chimes"

According to her love can touch everyone's tender heart who is open to all

> *"Out of these I pick the Lily*
> *Her friend is a Poppy, who is really silly.*
> *The naughty Lily who is white as milk*
> *Teased the Poppy, which is ruby silk. (The Lily and the Poppy)*

Every poem in this book of poetry has at least one of the five major elements used in poetry to depict goodness in life. Honorable Poet Dr. Liliyan Swarna Kalai. had sliced down each element to find the importance it brings to poetry.

> *"Heavenly to hear him say*
> *"I Love You"*
> *Even unuttered, his love's so true.*
> *It's 'the word' in every heart dwells*

How it enters, no one can tell.
All living beings feel love's dew
The moment love turns sour
Our world turns blue…." (A Love Poem)

Heaven is good. Hell is evil. The fact that God created mankind's soul with a divine entity and eternal destiny should have a significant impact on our choices and priorities in this short lifetime.

The benefits and splendor of heaven are greater than the punishments and tortures of hell. In the outer world, we are motivated to be happy, to be prosperous, to be loved, to be healthy, to be useful and creative in our work and to lead long, joyful lives.

In the inner world, we are motivated by truth, love and joy. When we take our power back from the outer world and place it where it belongs, at the center of our hearts, all the answers come clear. Everything in the nature become active and feels new life on the earth. The below poem is so simple, cute, but poetic.

"The bell rings
Class begins
Attendance taken
Students awaken
The lecture starts
For the troublesome lot
The front row stare

Backbenchers flare" (The Classroom)

To understand poetry, we must make sense of every single word to appreciate and enjoy the poem. There are many elements of a poem to be analyzed. In poetry, the poet might only exhibit a few of these elements in every poem. The first step to understanding poetry is to know the theme.

Theme is an idea that the poem expresses about the subject or uses the subject to explore a deeper thought. Letting the reader wonder and expand on their creativity and imagination. Another way to analyze a poem, besides knowing the theme, is to examine the impact the poem has on the reader. The emotional impact determines the tone and mood of the whole poem. It decides certain concepts.

I wish to congratulate Honorable Poet Dr. Liliyan Swarna Kalai. She has well penned and all verses are precisely depicted poetically too…Happy writing to her, and blissful reading to all readers

WILLIAMSJI MAVELI

Author

@ Whorled Wide Writers

CONTENTS

Celebrating Existence

Ever changing pictures on the never changing canvas

Where patterns are woven, knitted and painted

      Sketched and etched, crocheted and sculpted

Kaleidoscope set in dancing mosaics

Gold or silver, bronze or clay – black or white, colors

that are gay

Anything would go to make a song, story or play.

That tiny dot, a scratch or a blotch

Never out of place in the Master's Art.

Scenes unfolding on and off stage, behind the curtains,
under the blaze;

All take part to render a line,

      Orate, jest, stunt, blab or mime

The show goes on, even as players are changed – hauled,

shuffled, snatched and rearranged

Once the part is played, it's played no more

The Maker calls the shot and settles score.

Even the glow flies that dance across the light

Cheer dumbfounded in great delight.

The Unread Book

The book, so glossy and tactile;
It certainly outdid the pile
Sat on the shelf with a pleasant smile
Not one touched it even for a while
It sat there totally immobile
Only for decoration and style.

The contents were simple, cheerful and good
Lucid to convey the matter, as it should.
Very soon the new book would turn weary and old
Even the clear lines will be covered by mould.
Unaware of the votes it polled
It stayed put in the household.

It's a surprise why it was procured
Did the buyer in its beauty lured?
Or as a status symbol secured
Now turned to 'Kindle' which she adored
Oblivious to its fate the book endured
Its mystical future will be inured.

Liliyan Swarna Kalai

The Lily and the Poppy

It was a splendid garden
That resembles the Garden of Eden
Flowers with thousand hues you'll find
If you're really not colour blind.

Out of these I pick the Lily
Her friend is a Poppy, who is really silly.
The naughty Lily who is white as milk
Teased the Poppy, which is ruby silk.

Their day would start with a happy "'morning"
And always end with the Poppy mourning.
It's not the life it'll lose
But the Poppy's precious happy moods.

Games, pranks, teasing and about
Some riddle like 'Pick the odd one out'.
My! You should see the Poppy girl fret
She hasn't found a single answer yet.

Once the Lily asked the Silly,
Solve this one, at least half, if not fully.
Three ants, with their pants, went to a shrine.
One followed the other, in a very straight line.

A beetle coming from a casket
Met the first ant with the basket
Who said, there is an ant behind me
We'll talk sometime later when we see.

The second ant met the beetle
Whose horn was, as sharp as needle
Even this one likewise said and likewise fled
To the tomb of his mother who's dead.

The third ant saw the insect
Said, "Pardon me for my neglect
I'll see you when I'm free
For, there is an ant behind me".

"Well now my little Poppy Miss
Tell me now, how the ant said this
While all three were hustling
One after another among leaves rustling.

Boom a Bang a Bang!
The Poppy's head from left to right sprang
"No, I lose", said the innocent girl.
This made the Lily show her Pearls.

"Tis quite easy to solve it my child
For, the third ant told a lie".
No sooner than this was said
The Poppy hid her face to cry.

Mulberry my Irish setter

A cousin of mine urged me adopt, not a pup
He was a full grown dog.
Not trained in basic stuff and with his bark
There was no letup.
Always demanding love and food
Jumping, and circling
Chasing about everyone
 Ah! He was very crude.

Efforts to house train Mulberry - a herculean task
Yet, it's outcome rather faint.
Bothering all, unperturbed by the fracas
Happily he'd bask.
Many an attempt to pass him off, would tug at our heart
Somehow he stayed on and
Learnt to obey; 'no', 'shake a paw', 'come' and 'sit'
Made the fellow smart.

Rich chocolate brown, fur so silky
He was a darling
To all neighbours and sundry
His charming growl brought a cheer, even to a sulky.
The villain in the form of, another house pet
Jealous of the pampering he got
Made the other dog
Fume, snarl and break into a sweat.

Hoping he would learn to accommodate
Couple of years went by
No! Not a sign; the Alfa dog
Did not accord to constellate.
One ill-fated day they got into a fight
They rolled over and over each other
't was a vicious sight
Could ne'er figure out who got the worst bite.

In spite of efforts to bring down the poison
The giant dog did succumb
He breathed his last, my dear chum
Fell a prey to vile treason.
Two years of struggle, annoyance, impatience
Happiness, delight and amusement.
He suddenly left us
It's hard to find consolation.

Why, ah! Why I ask?
Did he enter this home and wring my heart
To live years two and
Only to be laid in a cask.
Wouldn't I had been better off
If I never had him at all
Than to be heavy laden
Every time I see his trough.

Liliyan Swarna Kalai

A Love Poem

Heavenly to hear him say
"I Love You"
Even unuttered, his love's so true.
It's 'the word' in every heart dwells
How it enters, no one can tell.
All living beings feel love's dew
The moment love turns sour
Our world turns blue.

God's great love sent me to this earth
He passed down love to mother at birth.
Her love showered on me is great
Impossible to measure; I have none to equate
Father's unbound love gave me a world of mirth
And help in build self-worth.

Blissful 'twas to hear him whisper 'My Sweetheart"
His rough hands' touch revealed his tender heart
Different was the world in his broadest chest
Through those burning eyes his passion I felt
Speak my love of our days of delight
If providence helps us unite.

Liliyan Swarna Kalai

Under Your Care

I talk tall, I act big
Think I am smart to even take a dig
At those around me, who are also very great;
Little discerning the furore, I create.
The things that I do, the angels wouldn't dare
But who am I Lord, without your care?

I gloat I've achieved – What? I cannot tell
I feel happy, why? I'm unable to spell
When I scrape a little inside of me
Oh, Lord I know, there's nothing to see.
If you turn fiery – Gee, I cannot bear
So please take me Lord, under your care.

I realize my Lord, I am a flower in the wild
Can stay fresh and pretty if the blowing wind is mild
Should a storm break and nature turn snare
I'll dart in Lord – right under your care.

Delonix Regia

(The Flame of the Forest)

She stood there, next to the building so tall,

Elegant, majestic and proud above all.

Away from lecture, my attention she would call

I wonder how she picks me, from so many in the hall.

Last term, she was bare and brown

Her naked self made me stare and frown

Bothering not, in my lessons I did drown

Till the day she wore her crown.

Liliyan Swarna Kalai

Last month she was dressed in green.

Her massive trunk made me dream,

How she'd look through the moon beam

Among all other trees would she gleam?

Now the Queen smiles at me

With the ruby crown she wears in glee

Graceful as a woman draped in a sari

Oh! The wingless, merry fairy!

Those Eyes............

Those eyes stared at me --------

        With indifference

When we met first;

I thought she was arrogant.

Those eyes stared at me---------

        With recognition

As we met next;

She was mindful I was there.

Liliyan Swarna Kalai

Those eyes stared at me -----------

    With a twinkle

When we knew each other

She was crazy and cute

Those eyes stared at me---------

    With a smile

We were in love;

I felt she was the happiest.

Those eyes stare at me----------

    ....This moment I realize

Those eyes are sad and full of tears.

The Classroom
(?)

The bell rings
Class begins

Attendance taken
Students awaken

The lecture starts
For the troublesome lot

The front row stare
Backbenchers flare

Chalk turn missile
The middle rows revile

Liliyan Swarna Kalai

War declared
Oppositions glare

Traitors grin
All of them win

The fighting is over
They all turn sober

The lecture goes on
Starting multiple yawns.

Thirty–Five

35

Turning thirty-five?

We all shall rejoice

And celebrate in tune of your choice!

My love proclaimed with so much zeal

I found it impossible to raise my voice.

What shall we have?

Cakes and candles, gifts and sweets

Friends to cheer you with tricks and treats

Ah! Do look forward to a special gift

Announced he, while planning the feast

Liliyan Swarna Kalai

How did it go?

Oh! He had my heart for the cake

Slicing it, with all that he spake

Candles did burn, scorching my soul

He gave me enough and more to take

Is that all?

His apathy added more to the day

When all that he meant fell into the Bay

'T is easy to set things right

For all it needs, is a SORRY anyway.

A Poem Dedicated to the Physically Challenged

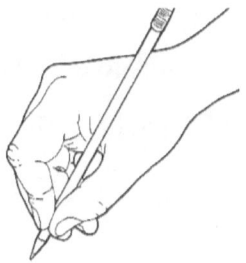

She saw –

> The world, through her bedroom window,
>
> The twenties and forties, hurrying and worrying
>
> Married and the harried, haughty and draughty;
>
> The needy and greedy, speedy and beady.

She thought –

> Of, what she saw through the window.
>
> The mother bird feeds the young ones' needs
>
> Hawkers cry, customers buy.
>
> Motorcars hoot, pickpockets loot.

She felt –

      Looking out her window, -

      Useless as a cripple; her thoughts went in ripple.

      She made up her mind, to tell mankind

      That in spite of her plight, SHE TOO COULD

WRITE!

Away from you

I wanted to run away from you
Right from the very start
What is holding me?
You pulling a string of my heart
In your presence I am merry

Yet, I need you to set me free.

Please let my heart go
You dwell without permit
For, it bleeds, do you know?
I'd pay any ransom for you to go.
If you think I'll be one more in your band

I suggest, you opt for a one-night stand.

Life isn't trouble-free
That is why I grope around
Surely I don't need this
What I want is a solid ground
You surely are one good thing that's happened to me

Unless you give me your heart, oh! Darling, I want to be free.

23

Yes, I feel your heart beat
You have one, I don't deny
To own you fully is not my feat
Treat me as a human; I want to cry
'T is not easy for me, to let you go

With a little help from you, I can, you know?

If you want to leave
Please take a part of me
It will help me grieve,
And pick up the pieces and flee
You find me amusing, so you use me for fun

Beloved, my feelings are true, that's why –

I WANT TO RUN

Angels are Real

They come in sight when you least expect
They are those you'll ne'er suspect.
Wingless, run of the mill guys who ne'er knew you
They all have faces; there are girls too.

In the middle of nowhere when you are stuck
In a tight spot or even a muck
In trouble, danger or a mess
Appears an angel – helps you in distress

A doctor, a patient or a teacher maybe
A maid or a mason even a traveller is she
At times a policeman, a friend indeed
Always show up in immense speed.

Some lend money to those in dire need.
Others bring medicine or mouths they'll feed
In flood, famine, pandemic or storm
Insider or outsider, they are all very warm

Utterly oblivious of the part they'd played
Their services mostly, would go unpaid.
Godsend are they, you have to concede
So bless them in your prayer and intercede

Regular is their day, ordinary their life
Going about their jobs through every day strife
In the given state, their role was ideal
And that's why I say, Angels are real.

Have a heart

It is not those precious stones
That lustrously adorns
The show window, I ask of you.
Not even a pretty thing
Nor a wedding ring,
I want from you
All I beg of you is to, Have a heart

 If you think, I can dance to your song
That is where you are wrong
For I crave to know your inner self
And nothing else.
So once again
I appeal to you – Have a Heart

If you spend your money
On stuff worth not a penny
You can always earn it back
If you utter a word, without care
Remember, it dangles in the air
You can never take it back
Afore you accuse me – Have a Heart

Magic Wand

If only I had a magic wand

Like fairy God mother blonde.

I would swing it in the air and quoit

Child abusers who sex exploit

Innocence of girl children

Plucked out of cradles, kindergarten,

From their own homes too; they like a shark

Rumple, squeeze and throw out as marc.

Would use the magic baton
On honour killers of bygone
Sodomites, persecutors, gangsters and
Pimps who are flesh hounds
And make them parade in the grounds.
Wonder if they would ever squirm
Like ugly, wriggly miserable worm.

Abortions are killing too since
It would make a normal person wince.
Alcoholics – their family they deform
Corruptions crumble social norm
Adultery kills mutual trust.
Blameless blood cry from dust
Culprits' deed must be bust.

Politicians suck like leech

Oath before land and God they breach

Hardworking, taxpaying peoples' money they loot.

Killers, peddlers of ill repute

Greedy, voracious and ghoulish brute.

Do they realize it's a curse

On Judgement Day they'll face the worst?

With the power to swing the magic rod

And use as I wish on these each sod

More I reflect on the horror of their deeds

Further I am irked to burn them as weeds

While the bailiff their crime reads

The magic will make them confess

And absolve - the world will be free of stress.

My Treasure Chest

Have a string of gems some precious and others semi
All qualified to be awarded year wise Emmy.
Want them graded as per their talent
Hmmm....oh, yes, some are quite gallant.

There are two 'Ayes'
One a doctor and very wise
We talk for hours on end
Right through the night; she's a good friend

The other a bureaucrat
Pushed me to greater height
I only have one 'Bee'
Who's as rare as brie

Learnt to handle money from 'Bee'
Albeit close, we ne'er got chummy.
Let me see the 'Cee'
Oh! She jumped fences you see

Still can credit her for the beauty tips
I save money from parlour trips.
'Gee' is next in line
For many years together we did dine

Taught me when to fight
Or when to fold up and take flight
'H' is after 'Gee'
She was full of glee

From class six, we journeyed on
Our pranks, fun and frolic are now gone
'Eye' is the one I'd better not say
No good about it so, best to stay away

'Kay's are like twin sisters
Good are they as twisters
Came in together and left one after another
With talents alike, my life they did smother

'Ell' of bygone years
Shared with me joys and tears
'Em' lifted me up when I was down
 I choose to bestow her the crown

The other 'Em'; means sweetness
Her culinary skills are a cut of uniqueness
She's a living witness for the lost
That offset her transplant cost.

The two 'Peas' not of one pod
First in line, I'd applaud
For soothing part in life she played
After her nuptials goodbye she bade.

Second 'Pea' inspired me
Even to write poetry.
'Aar' has my parents' name
 A senior in school; now chums we proclaim.

When we connect on the phone
Talk time meter gets blown
A gem is she; and would always spray
An aroma of harmony on her way.

'Yes'es there are five
First one keeps my spirits alive
Happens to be my travelling mate
Cruising, flying or driving; my soul she'd elate.

Liliyan Swarna Kalai

Three 'Yes'es were from my college class
Took me as their friend even though I'm a lass
One stood by me in days of dark
Gem he is; has made a mark.

The other 'Yes' honed me speak
A tongue in which I was weak
Next 'Yes', always locked horns
In politics and religion in any given form.

Last 'Yes' and one 'You' live in lands far away
Italian stood the test of time amidst life's screenplay
She taught to expand my perspective
Her sense of humour is incredibly infective.

'You' and I were together in class
She is capable of making me a laughing jackass
Together we had painted the town red
Cakes and doughnuts were our daily spread.

These string of gems I carefully cherish
Their role in my life made me flourish.
They stay in the chest, whether old or new
With them all, I surely have come through..

I know this is Heaven

Constantly I dream of Heaven!
On my accession
Sure many matters I'll not see.
They would mean nothing to me
Morning news paper full of gloom
No television set in my room
To yell of corruption, injustice, violence
Cheating and abuse – oh, no! Just peaceful silence
No human islands, made by devices
No media screaming of crisis

There's a Throne of God and the Lamb will rule
No hunger, panic and evil so cruel
Can be seen or heard in the realm
No swanky cars, jewels, to overwhelm
Nor business class flights or private jets
Can beget envy, yearning and lust for assets
Drugs and liquor, robbery and rape
Will find no place in this landscape
There'll ne'er be tragedy or disease
For the Heavenly Host holds the key.

What then is this Heaven I glance?
Did I see it happenstance?
Surely nay, for my Bible says
It is real and a glorious place
Shall wear robes of purity and righteousness
In my Father's mansion and in His graciousness
Will I dwell with great splendour and delight
For the King rules with love and might
The city needs no sun or moon to shine
For the glory of God emits light divine

When Christ the Lord says "Come Home" to me
With a hop, skip and jump I'll run to be
In His house where manors are many
There will I dwell for eternity.

The Banquet

You are invited on this day in the month of May
To partake with me a meal; please accept my appeal
Bring your spouse and your entire house
So reads the card; the recipients will be starred
They're people of great respect, I've carefully checked
Hence, starts preparation amidst great elation.

Budget planned, for an occasion so grand
Best star hotel booked; imposing it looked
Catering, menu and decors of venue
Fresh carnations to be placed at all stations
First-rate linen on which to dine in
Crockery vying for finesse with Cutlery

Hope all goes well, implore my every cell
Six course meal is the special deal
Amusements by Stars with drums and guitars
An array of lights, for the visitors' delight
Tables in order, cameras and recorder
To capture the event, of occasion well spent.

Every table with a server, to add fervour
A busser to care and wait with a flair
A captain to oversee with highest decree
Guests will be greeted; and with respect treated
Arranged chauffeured cars just for the cause
Table gifts placed in excellent taste

Now, for the guest list, so no one is missed
The hsouse cooks and maids of family and friends
Handy men all, who help us to mend
Conservancy workers of the nearby quarters
Gardeners and sweepers, and all housekeepers
Beggars and lepers and men of no letters

All receive the invite; their presence make the evening bright
There's no dress code; delightfully they all showed
In pink and blue and every other hue
Donned in their best, all were impressed
Children's eyes gleaming' older ones beaming
Looked around amazed as their minds appraised

After a while, they sat down with a smile
The delicious first course, went well with the work force
So were all others, up until desserts
At the end of it all they went out very tall
I stood there in delight, thanking each one for the night
Resolved to replicate; to them all I dedicate.

Liliyan Swarna Kalai

The Garden

Right in the middle of an urban jungle
An unassuming house, one would stumble
Has a garden not by design.
With an impending urge to redefine
I took a tour to investigate
As to what lies there within its gate

Garden crotons such as Joseph's coat,
Madagascar dragon tree,
Aloe Vera, fox tail fern amid other ferns, aplenty
Holy basil, Ficus, Coleus, Money plant
A mixture of Syngoniums, spider leaves plant,
Snake plant 'aka' mother in law's tongue
Have grown to be this garden's lung.

Ixora, Butterfly pea, Oleander, Musanda
Adenium, Euphorbia, Hibiscus, Alamanda
Jasmine, May flower, Lilies, Crossandra
Periwinkle, Bougainvillea and Gomphrena.
These flowering shrubs endured survival race
Have neither pattern nor landscape in limited space

Arrow head   bamboo, Papaya, Moringa
Pomegranate, Radish, Sapodilla
Banana, Eggplant, Mahogany
Spinach, Neem, Pennywort, Lemon tree,
Green chilli, Betel, Okra, Goose berry
And Coconut trees are absolutely sans topiary.

Even if not arty to human eye
Many a fauna my eye could spy
Tree Lizard, House Lizard, Bugs, Butterfly,
Beetle, Snail, Caterpillar, Frogs and Bee fly.
Bandicoot, Cat and an occasional Snake too
I happened to see Squirrels run through.

Liliyan Swarna Kalai

Birds find this place a delight
Crows, Sparrows and Koel birds
Use it as their campsite.
Pigeons, Woodpeckers, Mynas and Parrots
I could spot within the compound walls.
So, it isn't a quirky garden after all.